Otto Is Different

BY Franz Brandenberg

PICTURES BY James Stevenson

GREENWILLOW BOOKS NEW YORK

Library of Congress Cataloging in Publication Data

Brandenberg, Franz.
 Otto is different.
 Summary: Otto learns the advantages of being an octopus and having eight arms instead of only two. [1. Children's stories, American. [1. Octopus—Fiction]
I. Stevenson, James, (date), ill.   II. Title.
PZ7.B73640t 1985   [E]   84-13654
ISBN 0-688-04253-8
ISBN 0-688-04254-6 (lib. bdg.)

for BEAT

"Use your arms, Otto!" said Mother.
"I do," said Otto.
"But not all of them," said Mother.
"Oh, why do we have to be different!"
said Otto. "Why can't we be like
everyone else!"

"You should be happy to have
eight arms," said Father.
"Why?" asked Otto.
"Because you can do your work
four times faster than most of
your friends," said Father.
"That leaves you more time
to play," said Mother.
"Perhaps you are right," said Otto.

He brushed his teeth, tied his shoes,

washed his face, and blew his nose.

He set the table, and they
sat down to eat.
"Take your time," said Father.
"Mother told me to use all my arms,"
said Otto.
"But not when you are eating,"
said Mother. "After all, you have
only one mouth."

After the meal, Otto did his homework,

swept the floor, and practiced the piano.

"You see," said Mother. "Thanks to your eight arms you are already finished." Otto buttoned up his sweater and went out to play.

His friends weren't there yet.
He had time for a game of hockey
all by himself.

When his friends finally arrived,
they fought over him.
Both teams wanted him to be
their goalie.

So he first played for one team,
and then for the other.
The team he was on always won.

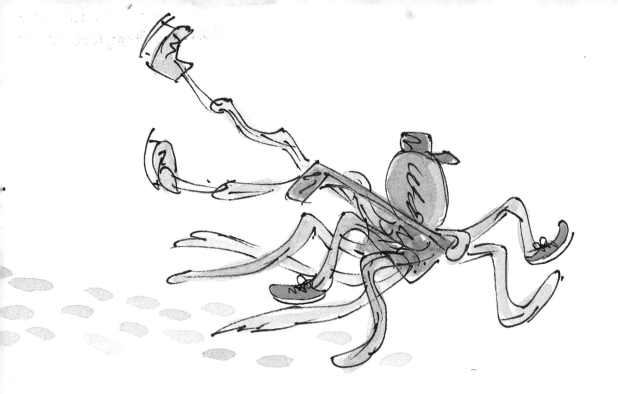

When Otto got home Father said,
"Do you still want to be like everyone else?"
"If I were like everyone else, only two arms
would be tired instead of eight," said Otto.

"And instead of getting hugged good night
with eight arms," said Mother, "you'd
get hugged with only two."
"And so would you," said Otto.